MW00935788

SPY DOGS # 3
The Aliens Invasion

Amma Lee

Copyright © 2015 Author Name

All rights reserved.

ISBN-13: 9781517205164

Introduction

Puggy and Mannie are back in their last adventure to take on the aliens once and for all. In the beginning of the series in "A Suspicious Neighbor," Puggy first made contact with an alien who had moved in next door to him. This alien, Cyze, had captured animals to experiment on so that he could control them to do whatever he asked of them.

A new alien was introduced in "Cat's Revenge" as Zork, who had taken up residence at a blue house a few blocks from Puggy to help Cyze with the experiments on the animals. In book one, due to fate, Puggy was modified with advanced technology which led him to become a spy. Saving Mannie, his Jack Russel friend, in book one, Mannie begins showing his true worth and after becoming modified in book two, Mannie is now a key player in "The Aliens Invasion."

In "The Aliens Invasion," the aliens were not easy to find this time because they had left the blue house and disguised themselves as humans. To make matters worse, they had figured out how to control the animals completely! Puggy and Mannie knew that they wouldn't stand a chance against the animals so they needed a plan that involved not fighting the animals, but having the animals fight for them.

But what's this? Puggy appears to have come down with a dreadful illness and is unable to perform to the best of his abilities. It seems like after this everything started to go downhill fast and more problems started to arise. It was up to Mannie now to try to save the day while Puggy was on the sideline giving the animals instructions on what was needed to be done.

Chapter One

Puggy ran around a few minutes outside with Bill before he had to go to work. Bill made it his top priority to spend some time with Puggy before he went to work because he would be exhausted after he came back home. Puggy enjoyed this change in Bill and he began thinking that Bill was trying his hardest to make sure that Puggy didn't feel lonely. It had been a month since the cat "ran" away and Bill had convinced himself that Puggy was sad.

"Alright Puggy," Bill said after he threw the Frisbee for the last time. "I need to head out to work. You can stay outside for a little while, but don't go anywhere else." Puggy barked and wagged his tail. Bill had a feeling that Puggy went other places while he was outside when Bill wasn't around, but he couldn't prove it.

Puggy barked and jumped onto Bill's pants leg while Bill ruffled his fur. "Be a good boy," Bill said and walked towards his car. He waved at Puggy before he drove off and in a matter of seconds; Puggy was unable to see him anymore. Instead of going back inside to go to his office that he made for himself in the attic, he waited for little Mannie to round the corner.

Puggy and Mannie had been working together as partners for the last month in order to find out a way to defeat the aliens for good. Mannie was modified just like Puggy which made him a great partner. When Mannie's owner left for work, Mannie would make his way over to Puggy and they'd go into the attic to do some research. Puggy waited patiently for Mannie to arrive.

After several long minutes of waiting, Puggy heard Mannie bark as he approached the house. Puggy barked too, his way of greeting his friend, and led him into the house. Mannie stopped into the kitchen at first and after whining, Puggy barked, allowing Mannie to eat some of his leftover food. His owner had forgotten to put some food out for him because she was in a hurry that morning. Once Mannie had his fill, he followed Puggy into the attic.

For an hour or two, Puggy and Mannie looked through the files for information that they might have missed in their earlier review. They found many things that led them to believe that the aliens were onto something and that they were incredibly close with having the alien invasion happen. There had been several communications between them and aliens from outer space. It looked like Zork and Cyze were sending transmissions out of the house.

Puggy noticed that they discovered the formula to make the animals more like Puggy and Mannie. Mannie asked if they had experimented on him and Mannie continuously answered no. Puggy could not determine how Mannie had undergone the modification, but if he had to make a guess it was possible that some of the formula must have fell on him somehow.

Puggy concluded that his very own modification were impossible for him to figure out exactly how it had happened. He just brushed it off and said that it was fate that made it happen for him. Puggy and Mannie took turns searching through the information and they both decided that the information needed to be destroyed once they were able to decode the things that they were unsure about. If this information got into the wrong hands, like the aliens again, they wouldn't be able to prevent the devastation that would surely happen.

When they were tired and ready to call it a day, they looked out of the window and noticed that it was getting rather late. Mannie needed to get back home before his owner came back and realized he was gone. Puggy opened the hatch to the main floor and they jumped through it with ease. Puggy nodded his head as Mannie ran quickly through the animal entrance, almost too fast to the normal eye. A few seconds after Mannie left, Bill opened the door.

"Hey boy, were you waiting for me?" Bill said walking

through the door. Puggy greeted Bill with a bark and ran into the kitchen. "I know that you're hungry. I'm sorry that I'm so late." Puggy could have fixed his own bowl, but he didn't want to risk Bill noticing his food bag was lower than when he had left home. Puggy also did not want to be scolded.

Bill poured the food into his bowl and Puggy rushed over to it. Bill had to take his hand away quickly so that Puggy wouldn't think it was food. "Wow, what have you been doing today? You're practically starving." Just like Bill, Puggy had worked all day as well. Puggy was sure that he felt as exhausted as Bill looked. They both had jobs to do and unfortunately for Puggy, his job had higher stakes.

Bill walked into the living room after he had fixed his plate. He wanted to watch a little TV because it felt like the only thing he's done recently was work. Puggy joined him on the couch and watched TV with him in silence. Nodding off a little, Bill began changing the channels. Puggy whined and knocked the remote out of his hand, causing the channel to stop on the news station.

"A few months ago we covered the story of neighborhood dogs going missing, which police are still investigating into this." Puggy's ears shot up once he heard her speaking about the missing dogs. "However, it seems that the strings of disappearances are beginning to happen again, but with people."

Puggy couldn't believe what he was hearing. It appeared

that two people had suddenly vanished from their homes without a trace. Puggy began barking.

"Puggy, don't bark so loud at night." Bill rubbed his eye and looked down at Puggy. Puggy was on the couch staring intently at the TV screen, bending down, Bill grabbed the remote and turned the TV off.

Angered by this, Puggy jumped off of the couch and began barking louder. "Don't give me any of that." Bill said and pointed in the direction of the bedroom. "Time to go to bed," Puggy whined but made his way into the bedroom.

Bill followed closely behind him, but he made a left towards the bathroom instead of continuing straight. Puggy jumped onto the bed and lied down; he wanted to watch a little more of the report to see if he could get any clues that pointed toward the aliens being the culprits. Puggy knew in his heart that Zork and Cyze were able to escape the cages that Mannie and Puggy put them into.

Puggy and Mannie tried not to monitor the house too much out of fear that people would become suspicious, but they did sneak a peek through the window once a week. Neither Puggy nor Mannie was able to check it that week, so it was a strong possibility that they were out of their cages. It was decided that he'd take Mannie and they'll check out the blue house that next morning. Puggy closed his eyes and drifted off to sleep.

Chapter Two

Puggy was startled out of his sleep when he felt
something licking his face. When his eyes adjusted to
the darkness, he was shocked to find Mannie standing in
front of him on the bed. Puggy looked behind him at
Bill, he was snoring loudly which meant that he was in a
deep sleep. He jumped off of the bed with Mannie and
made their way softly into the living room. Puggy knew
that Mannie saw the news report before he even asked.

Mannie began whimpering, he was worried about the
animals and the missing humans. Puggy was also
worried so they decided to check in on the aliens. It was
dark and chilly outside as they flew in silence to the blue
house. Mannie was still getting used to his powers, so he
didn't fly as quickly as Puggy did, but Puggy was patient
and didn't leave him behind. It took them longer than
they had wanted, but they made it safely to the house.

Puggy barked softly as he told Mannie to land with

caution. Mannie did what he was told and landed onto the ground without any incidents. When they made it to the front door, they were surprised to find it bolted shut. They definitely didn't do this and finding the door in that state alarmed them. Mannie wanted to pry it up, but Puggy shook his head because that'll make too much noise and would disturb the neighbors.

They went under the porch to look through the window and they were surprised by what they saw. They saw nothing! Everything was gone: the animals, the computers, the aliens, there was nothing left behind! Puggy whimpered in despair, he knew that the aliens had gotten loose, but finding out that he was right hurt him deeply. Mannie rested one of his paws onto his back to try and console Puggy. They'd save the humans and animals in no time.

Mannie suggested that they fly over the city in search of the aliens. Puggy thought that was a good idea, so they split up. They searched the city for hours, using their scanners to pick up odd heat waves, but they found nothing. They met back up in front of Bill's house just as the sun began rising. They were both tired and needed to get some sleep. They agreed to meet back up later and Mannie ran off in the direction of his home.

Puggy snuck back into the house and got back onto the bed, it was six in the morning and he knew that he had two more hours to sleep before Bill woke up. He closed his eyes but quickly learned that he would not be able to fall asleep. The aliens definitely had another trick up their sleeves and he hated that he waited to act on his intuition. Instead of going to sleep earlier that night, he should have checked in on that house. The aliens might have still have been there.

Puggy looked back at Bill as he slept peacefully. He was glad that they weren't able to get their hands on Bill, but that didn't mean that he wanted other people to be hurt. He knew that there was a strong possibility to save the animals, but could he save a human that had their bodies taken over? He'd have to revisit the aliens' files to see if they had any information on how they took over a human's body. He didn't think he'd find anything, but it was worth a try.

When Bill's alarm clock rung at 8:15, Puggy was still up thinking about what he could do to make things right. Bill jumped out of bed and looked at Puggy once he noticed that he was awake. "You're up early" he said as he made his way to the bathroom. Considering that Puggy had yet to fall asleep, he was up pretty late. Puggy watched Bill each morning brewing a dark liquid, which he learned was called 'coffee'. It apparently helped people stay awake and Puggy felt like he'd fall out at any moment.

Bill wiped his face as the coffee began dribbling down his face. "There's nothing quite like a hot cup of coffee to get a man through the day." If that was true, Puggy would definitely have to make himself a cup. Bill poured some dog food into Puggy's bowl and made his way out the door. "See you later," he called out just before closing it. Forgetting about the food, Puggy walked over to the coffee pot and lucky enough for him, there was still some left.

Puggy's metal pole extended out of his body and created a hand. He reached for his water bowl and dumped it into the sink and poured coffee into it in the water's place. Puggy thought that since coffee helped Bill stay awake during the day that it'll surely help him. The liquid was hot as he stuck his tongue inside of the bowl. It was bitter, but Puggy drunk all of it. He didn't feel any better after he drunk it; in fact, he began to feel sleepier and somewhat weaker.

Maybe drinking something aimed at humans wouldn't help Puggy at all; it appeared to have had the opposite effect. Puggy shook his head, he was sure that the effects would wear off in a few hours. Puggy walked abnormally slowly towards the door so that he could meet Mannie outside. His legs felt heavy and his breathing came out rough, but he kept telling himself that he was fine. Before Puggy was able to make it towards the door, Mannie ran straight in.

Mannie looked at his friend in curiosity as Puggy slowly came over to him. Mannie was worried that he was sick, so he ran into the kitchen, grabbed his bowl and poured some fresh water into it. Whenever he was feeling ill, drinking water always made him feel better. Puggy thought it was a good idea so he drunk all of his water and hoped that he would begin feeling better. Puggy started feeling a little better after a few minutes, but he still wasn't his best.

The two of them went to Puggy's "office" to discuss possible reasons to why they couldn't detect the aliens. Puggy had a hard time keeping himself alert and could hardly think correctly. Mannie didn't seem to notice as he continued to explain his findings. It took Puggy a while to understand what Mannie was saying, but when he did, he thought that Mannie was making a lot of sense.

Mannie suggested that the aliens used the humans' bodies that they acquired to shield their alien presence, so if they wanted to find the alien, they'll need to use their modifications to locate the missing men. Puggy moved over so that Mannie could use the computer. Puggy wasn't at his best at the moment so he felt that Mannie would do a better job at finding the information that they needed.

Mannie looked up the news report that reported the humans missing and memorized their names. Using advance software, Mannie was able to look up their addresses. The plan was for them to go over to these kidnapped human's homes and take something of theirs that has their scent on it. From there, Puggy and Mannie could use these objects to look for matching DNA with their scanners.

Mannie looked over at Puggy and saw that he wasn't as relaxed as he normally was. Mannie believed that Puggy wasn't fit for this mission today and Mannie didn't want to do it alone because he was still getting use to his modifications. Puggy objected several times insisting that he'd be able to carry out the mission, but Mannie shook his head.

Saving the animals and the world was important, but they wouldn't be able to save anyone if Puggy wasn't at his best. Puggy whined but he listened to Mannie. He would only get in the way so they decided to look for them tomorrow.

Mannie nodded his head at Puggy and made his way through the animal entrance. Puggy watched Mannie until he was out of sight and made his way to the bedroom. He'd made a grave mistake when he decided to consume human food which resulted in them having to hold back on saving the animals and humans for another day. Puggy slept, but it was an uneasy rest because he kept thinking that everything would go wrong just because of his illness.

Chapter Three

"Puggy! Puggy!" Puggy stirred when he heard Bill calling his name. Opening one eye, he glanced in Bill's direction. Bill had a concerned expression on his face. "What's wrong?" Bill reached out and stroked Puggy's head. He didn't feel better, but he didn't want Bill worrying about him. With a lot of effort, he jumped up quickly and barked as normally as possible. His bones ached when he did that, but it put a smile on Bill's face. "Whew, I thought something was wrong with you. I guess dogs' needs naps sometimes too."

Puggy was shocked that he had managed to sleep all day, it were so unlike him. He couldn't believe that he had slept all the way till Bill got home and he was still tired! Bill poured Puggy some food into his bowl and refilled his water bowl. "You must have been really thirsty today. Your bowl is empty." Puggy didn't feel like eating anything, but he welcomed the water that was sat down in front of his face. Instead of walking away,

Bill stayed behind and watched him.

Kneeling down in front of Puggy, Bill grabbed his face. "You look okay, but you're acting weird." Bill said as he looked Puggy in his eyes. Even though Puggy was sick, it wasn't like he could up and tell Bill that he wasn't feeling good, he was still a dog after all. Bill pushed his head from side to side, looking in his ears, in his mouth for possible objects that might be hurting Puggy, but he couldn't find anything.

"I might have to take you to the vet." If dogs could go pale, Puggy would have gone pale at that moment. He couldn't let Bill take him to the vet because they'd find out that Puggy wasn't normal. It was possible that they'd try to experiment on him as well and he'd be all over the news.

He needed to keep his abilities a secret because if normal people knew, they'd make his and Bill's lives difficult. Puggy wagged his tail and put on his "normal" performance. Bill wasn't entirely convinced, but he stopped talking about the vet for the moment.

Bill had apparently gone out that night with some coworkers and got something to eat. Bill watched Puggy for a while before he decided to go into his room to get ready for bed. Puggy knew that if he didn't eat at least some of his food, Bill would grow suspicious again. So with a heavy heart, Puggy began eating his food. Each bite that he chewed made him sicker and sicker, but he continued to eat and he didn't stop until his food was completely gone.

When Puggy went into the room thirty minutes later, Bill was already snoring. He jumped back onto the bed, but this time he lied on his side instead of his stomach. He was full and he feared the worst if he lied on his stomach. He drifted back to sleep, still feeling the negative effects from the coffee.

Puggy woke up the next day with something wet pushing into his face. When he woke up, he was surprised to see Mannie there again. Puggy still wasn't feeling well, but he didn't want to tell Mannie. He jumped up as happily as he could manage and barked loud. Mannie barked as well when he saw that his friend was okay and ran towards the front door.

Puggy's body still felt weak, but he ran to the door pretending that nothing was wrong. Mannie exited the door and began flying.
When Puggy went outside and commanded his body to create a device to help him fly, he was taken aback by how slow his modification was working. Normally his metal poles would shoot out quickly, but today they barely wanted to extend from his body. Feeling Mannie's eyes on him, he begged his body to listen to him and it finally did. In no time, Puggy was in the air beside Mannie.

They found the first man's house with ease because he lived up the street from Mannie. The man was name George Stevens who was a carpenter. When they managed to get inside his house, Puggy and Mannie scanned his work uniform and pulled up his DNA.

The next house they went to belong to a Kevin Burden. He was a painter and his house was filled with art supplies. Puggy found an overused paint brush and they took turns scanning it. After they got enough information from the house, they took to the sky again.

They took out their scanners again and this time they flew around together instead of separate. They knew that they'd definitely find them today and they were right! Their scanners locked in on two humans' whose DNA's matched the missing men.

The bad part about it was the aliens were located on the other side of the city so they'd have to make this quick before their owners got back home. Puggy and Mannie landed on the ground with ease, well Mannie landed with ease, Puggy found the task to be a bit hard.

Making their way to the window they looked inside. The house looked perfectly normal. They went under the porch and the basement was normal as well. Puggy was confused; the aliens had always used the main floor and basement to house all of their materials. Why did they change now? Mannie barked softly and Puggy was taken out of his thoughts. He didn't even realize that Mannie had left his side. Mannie was flying near the roof of the house and he had a serious look on his face.

With great effort Puggy was able to fly towards the top

of the house and he was petrified to see George and
Kevin with red eyed dogs surrounding them. Puggy or
Mannie couldn't tell who Zork was and who Cyze was,
but they knew that they were the humans in disguise.

Puggy was extremely hurt to see that they had somehow
managed to control the animals, but he was thankful that
their bodies were still enclosed in metal. It is possible
that the aliens didn't know that they had created the
substance to allow the animals to become modified from
inside of their bodies instead of out. Puggy and Mannie
was glad about this because it'll be easier to break their
control if they could see their device.

Puggy and Mannie watched the dogs obey the aliens'
every command and they were worried about how good
they had gotten with their controls. Puggy and Mannie
knew it'll be difficult to take on all of the dogs so they'd
have to avoid having a confrontation with them. Mannie
noticed that the aliens could only control them when
they were holding the control pad. So it was possible
that whoever had the control device would be able to
control them.

Puggy was shocked about how observant Mannie was
when it came to the aliens. Lately, Puggy wasn't even
able to figure out the simplest of things. He was starting
to think that he was losing his intelligence. He quickly
shook his head. His illness was preventing him from
thinking properly; he just needed to get back to normal
as soon as possible.

They watched the aliens for a long while before they decided that they were not going to leave the attic, so that meant that they needed to sneak in from the main floor. Puggy didn't like this idea, but it was the only suggestion that they had. Puggy tried to create a laser with his metal poles, but he kept creating hands, which frustrated him.

Mannie quickly went to Puggy's aid and made a laser. Puggy barked his thanks at Mannie and he grabbed the glass just before it went crashing onto the ground. After a few attempts for Puggy to get through the window, Mannie had made the hole too small, Puggy was finally through.

They snuck their way through the house amazed that the aliens left the first floor unchanged. Mannie suggested that perhaps they did it that way so that they wouldn't be able to find their location and Puggy had to admit that was definitely a plausible reason. He was happy that Mannie was solving all of their problems, but he was upset that he wasn't able to add any input himself. When they made it up to the attic, they stood near the entrance door and listened and what they heard was terrible!

Chapter Four

"We did it Zork!" George said with a huge grin on his face. Well at least Puggy and Mannie knew who was who. Zork, who was using Kevin's body, grinned from ear to ear.

"Yes brother," Zork said as he raised his hands and the dogs barked in unison. "We have enough intelligence to conquer Earth!" What Zork had said really gotten under his skin and before he was able to manage an intelligent thought, Puggy went flying into the room barking. Mannie was surprised that Puggy went in before discussing it with each other, but he followed behind cautiously. The aliens gasped when they saw the two dogs, but they grinned after getting over the initial shock.

"We knew it was a matter of time till you found us." Cyze said as his grin began widening. "You're too late now. We have all of the information that we need to take over this world."

Puggy growled and went in to pounce on Cyze, but Mannie stopped him with a powerful bark. Neither Puggy nor Mannie knew what the aliens' had up their sleeves; Mannie also had to remind Puggy that the aliens were using the bodies of the humans they were trying to rescue.

"Smart dog," Zork said as he walked over to the modified dogs who were staring at Puggy and Mannie in anger. "At the push of this button" Zork said holding up a remote so that Puggy and Mannie could see, "These dogs would attack you until they're the last ones standing!" Cyze laughed as he walked over closer to Puggy and Mannie.

"From the looks of you," Cyze said looking over Puggy's body. "You wouldn't be able to defeat them anyways. You're not looking well at all." Puggy howled. How were the aliens able to see through his disguise? He was still sick, but he thought that he was hiding his illness well.

Mannie looked over at Puggy and whined. He wasn't sure earlier because Puggy was acting normal, but now that the alien brought it up, he could definitely tell that Puggy wasn't alright.

"Move and I'll tell the dogs to attack!" Zork said walking closer to Puggy. Puggy growled, he knew that they were right, Puggy and Mannie probably didn't stand a chance against the aliens and the dogs. Puggy flinched when a light pierced his eyes and he grew still when he heard Zork gasp. "The dog's modification is wearing off!" Zork said as he reviewed the data that was coming across the screen of the device he was using. Cyze walked over to Zork and looked. He broke out in laughter.

"Well... Well... Well... It looks like we won't have to worry about little Puggy at all." Puggy didn't understand what they were saying. What was the cause of him losing his power? He hadn't done anything different.

He looked over at Mannie and whined. If the aliens were telling the truth, he wouldn't be able to save the animals. Puggy wouldn't be able to battle the aliens and they would ultimately take over the world and worse, take Bill.

Cyze looked at the device that Zork was holding until he finally understood why Puggy's powers were weakening. "It looks like the little doggy ate something that he shouldn't have." Puggy growled. That was impossible! He ate the same food that Bill fixed him every day, but then a thought crossed his mind. The coffee! When Puggy drunk the coffee, he had started feeling weak and his abilities weren't acting quite correctly.

"Ah. I see," Zork said once he saw exactly what Cyze was saying. His grinned matched his brother's. "Whatever this dog ate weakened his bones which are where his modification lies. It's breaking his modifications down at an alarming rate. He will be back to a normal dog in a matter of minutes"

No! Puggy couldn't lose his powers just as they were so close to defeating the aliens. He couldn't let the aliens win. In an act of desperation, Puggy leapt at Zork and knocked the remote out of his hands.

Puggy was thankful that the dogs only reacted when they were told to do so. Cyze ran over to try and grab the device but Mannie was quick on his heels. Mannie and Puggy barked in unison as their anger washed over them. Mannie was hurt that Puggy was losing his abilities and that he was saddened about it.

Mannie was also angry that the aliens found his friend's pain humorous. Zork was able to throw Puggy off of him because since Puggy was losing his strength, Zork was becoming stronger than Puggy. Zork grabbed the remote quickly before Mannie went for him.

"Attack!" Zork screamed and the dogs took off running. In that instant, Mannie knew that they had to get out of there. He left Cyze's side and went straight for Puggy. Mannie's modification was still more advanced than the animals, so he got to Puggy quicker. Hands shot out of his body and he grabbed Puggy as soon as his hands were close enough to reach him. Two more poles shot out of his body which gave him wings.

Puggy was whimpering with pain, but he still tried to

help his friend in any way that he possibly could. When a dog leapt in the air towards Puggy and Mannie, he commanded that his poles create claws. Puggy could feel the poles trying their best to poke through his skin, but they refused to. He tried a few more times, but he realized that his powers had left him. At that moment of realization, the dog closer to them crashed into them.

When Puggy opened his eyes, after apparently hitting his head on the floor, he was in awe to see Mannie battling all of the dogs. Several poles extended from Mannie's body and each one was attacking the numerous dogs surrounding him. Puggy was weak but he made himself stand up on all four legs. He couldn't let Mannie fight alone because even though he wasn't modified anymore; he appeared to have kept his intelligence.

The animals didn't appear to have noticed that he was up or they decided not to pay him any mind. Either way, it was good enough for Puggy. Puggy limped to the corner and waited for an opening to be presented to him. Puggy saw the aliens laughing and clapping from the stairs and that really made Puggy angry.

Cyze had the remote now, he'll attack as soon as he found the best moment. When Mannie howled after he got bitten by one of the dogs, Puggy saw Cyze and Zork double over laughing. Now was his chance. Using his normal dog's agility, Puggy ran over to the aliens and just as they noticed him approaching, he jumped up and bit the remote out of Cyze's hand.

"Give that back here!" Cyze yelled but Puggy ran over to the other side of the room. Puggy felt some of his strength returning, probably because the modification was flushed out of his system. Puggy examined the remote for a moment, placed it on the floor and pressed the button with his nose while barking. All of the animals stopped what they were doing and turned to Puggy and they barked in unison. The animals were now under Puggy's control.

"We can't have them ruining our plans. Call for back-up!" Zork screamed as Cyze and he ran back upstairs to the attic. Puggy was going to press the button again and have the animals attack them when a loud ear splitting noise surrounded the house and Puggy was sure that other people could hear it as well. All of the animals, Puggy and Mannie included, howled as the noise irritated their ears. They needed to find a way to stop the noise before the whole city heard it!

Chapter Five

People began coming out of their houses and exiting their vehicles when they heard the strange alarm. At first they thought it was a tornado coming their way, but it was a beautiful day with not a single cloud in the sky. A young boy riding his bike stopped in the middle of the road and pointed towards the sky. "Look at that up there!" he yelled and everyone's eyes followed his hand.

People began gasping when they noticed a large dark shape forming in the sky. "What is that?"

More people began stopping and looking at the foreign object with interest. Several long minutes passed before the people saw a small circular hole opening up with a beautiful green light coming from it. They found it mesmerizing and people started walking directly under the object.

The neighborhood kids were happy to see the object

because of the pretty lights. However, what happened next would be the event to change everyone's lives. That same beautiful green light shot towards the street, melting the ground directly in front of Bill's car.

"Our brothers are finally here!" Zork shouted as he heard the chaos begin outside. Mannie got up off of the floor once his ears stopped ringing and looked towards Puggy. Puggy's legs were shaking hard, but he appeared to have been alright.

"This is the end!" Cyze shouted laughing evilly. It was too late for Mannie and Puggy to stop the aliens from entering the earth, but it wasn't impossible for them to defeat the aliens. Puggy pushed the button again with his nose and barked. The animals were now his to control!

Puggy told the dogs to capture Cyze and Zork and after that they'd go outside to battle the aliens. Zork and Cyze didn't stand a chance against the animals and they were taken down quite easily. Their capture didn't hurt their mood, however.

"We don't care whatever you do to us," Zork began still laughing. "We've won!" Mannie was tired of all of the aliens' arrogant confidence. Producing a spray bottle with his metal poles, Mannie sprayed both of them in the face and they fell quickly asleep. Once they had gotten that out of the way; Mannie, Puggy, and the modified animals sped through the door. Puggy was noticeably slower than the rest of them, but he kept up a good pace.

He couldn't help them fight, but he could give them advice.

The alien's ship was so big that it covered the entire sky around their small city. Men, women and children were running and cars were left behind. Mannie looked at the city in horror. How could a city so beautiful go into ruins so quickly? He'd never forgive the aliens for what they had done. Puggy instructed the animals to get as high as possible since their modifications didn't allow them to fly.

Mannie led the group, flying heads on into the space ship. Mannie would take the ship's middle so that it'll be unable to shoot out the acid and the animals would take out their sides. Puggy barked, telling everyone to get into place. Once they were aligned, Puggy howled and the animals went in for the attack.

Puggy hated the attention that they dogs were getting, their powers were supposed to have been a secret, but one couldn't be secretive in a situation like this. Some of the younger humans even stopped running and took pictures of the animals.

"Is that dog flying?" Puggy heard a female's voice say. Puggy had to think of a way to rebuild the entire city and wipe out their memories by the time they were done. As the animals moved closer to the spaceship, Puggy realized that he needed to move closer.

He ran towards a spot filled with a lot of cars, which was a good place for him to take cover, when he began coughing when he saw a familiar car. It was Bill's car! Was he outside in this madness? Was he okay? Puggy needed to find Bill before any more damage happened.

Before he ran off in search for Bill, Puggy barked out his instructions to his team. When they nodded signaling that they understood, Puggy took off running towards Bill's car. Puggy needed Bill's scent so that he'd be able to track him down quicker. Once Puggy had Bill's scent in his memory, he pressed his nose to the ground and ran towards Bill's scent.

Puggy had to constantly dodge debris that was flying all around him. He looked up into the sky amazed at how far the spaceship was extending out. He saw the ship shaking, signaling that the animals were damaging it greatly. Bringing his attention back to the task at hand, he picked up his pace once Bill's scent had grown stronger.

While Puggy was gone, Mannie led the team of animals the best way that he could. He wasn't a leader like Puggy, but he had the technology to research appropriate tactics. Mannie's powers allowed him to copy the signal that the remote control that Puggy used to control the animals. He was happy for having this skill since Puggy had the remote with him. He felt bad for doing this, but they needed the animals on their side.

Mannie continuously damaged the middle where the

ship's weapon was at. The aliens who were controlling the ship made several attempts to shoot at Mannie, but Mannie dodged each of their beams with ease. Mannie's opponents were persistent, but each time they tried to use their beam, he'd pierce the object with his own. The ship's defenses and offenses were weakening, though this was a long battle, he knew that with the help of all of the animals, they'd surely be victorious!

Once Mannie had damaged the middle enough so that the aliens wouldn't be able to shoot their beams, he went over to the sides to help his companions. The dogs were having a more difficult time, since they were unable to fly, but they did damage the ship a bit.

Changing his poles to a metal hammer, Mannie pounded away at the sides. He flew all around the ship helping each of the animals, but the aliens in the ship apparently had a plan B. On the sides of the ship, metal spikes and blades extended from out of it. The aliens controlling the ship were trying to make it more difficult for the animals to move closer to it.

Mannie whined because he knew that the blades and the spikes would damage his poles. He barked commanding the animals to cease their attacks. The animals made their way back to the ground and Mannie stood there looking at the ship uncomfortably. He couldn't think of a way to overcome this predicament.

He knew that Puggy had gone to find and save Bill, but Mannie needed him back now. Communications between the two would be incredibly hard since Puggy wasn't modified anymore. Mannie did the only thing that he could think of; he howled hoping that Puggy would hear his distress call.

Chapter Six

Puggy ran through the almost unrecognizable city until he came across someone lying on the ground. He whined in horror when he recognized the man as being Bill! He ran to him and licked his face. Puggy was so afraid that Bill was hurt and didn't know what he'd do if he was. After a quick inspection of Bill's unconscious body, Puggy realized that Bill probably just fainted from the horror of the situation.

Other than dirt and a few small scratches, Bill was completely fine. Puggy needed to move Bill quickly so that nobody would accidently step on him while they were running. Puggy bit at Bill's shirt and with a lot of effort and determination, he began dragging Bill to a safer spot.

At that very moment, Puggy wished that he had his modifications because then he wouldn't have struggled as much as he did. It took Puggy fifteen minutes to drag Bill across the street, but he finally managed to pull Bill under a bench. The bench was deep inside of the concrete so Puggy was confident that the bench couldn't be easily moved.

Running over to a nearby newsstand, Puggy grabbed some newspapers into his mouth and ran back to Bill. It wasn't much, but he wanted to protect Bill from some of the wind and from being detected.

Licking Bill's face, Puggy was saddened that he'd have to leave him there for a while, but he needed to get back to his friends and stop the aliens' attack. Just as he thought this, Mannie's howls pierced his ears. They were in trouble! Puggy looked at Bill one more time before he ran off. He needed to get to his friends fast because they needed his help.

Puggy ran faster than any normal dog could have possibly managed. When Puggy arrived back on the scene, he was surprised to see the dogs not attacking the spaceship any longer. He was more surprised to see them on the ground looking up at the spaceship, Puggy barked once he was closer to them.

Mannie turned around quickly and ran closer to his friend. He told Puggy what had happened and how the aliens made it almost impossible to get close to the ship. Mannie also told him that he knew his metal poles would not last against the ship's spikes and blades.

Puggy wasn't surprised that the aliens thought of a way to protect their ship if it came under attack. Looking at how fast the blades moved, Mannie was right; his modifications wouldn't be able to touch them. Looking around to see if he saw something that they could use in their favor, Puggy barked when he saw just the material. Mannie listened to Puggy's idea and he jumped in glee.

Puggy saw several large trees lying on the ground in front of them. If they cut the tree trunks into smaller pieces, they should be able to ram the sticks between the blades, which should stop them for a few moments. Puggy ran over to the fallen trees and pushed them towards the animals where they went quickly to work by cutting them into smaller pieces.

Once they had finished that, Mannie told the animals to get ready on his mark. Mannie counted down from three and Mannie soared in the air and rammed the stick in between the blade as Puggy instructed. Puggy's plan worked and the blades stopped long enough for Mannie to destroy them with his laser beam. Each of the animals followed Mannie's example and stopped the blades that they were handling.

Mannie flew around to each of the stopped blades and destroyed them with his lasers. Puggy and Mannie howled in joy once the blades were taken care of. Puggy was so happy that his intelligence hadn't left them. He didn't think Mannie or the other animals would have been able to figure that out.

Puggy pushed the button on the remote with his nose and asked the animals to return to him. Once they were all present, he told them to find an opening in the ship and force their way inside to capture the aliens. They barked loudly and took off. Puggy watched the animals trying to find the entrance, but they could not.

Puggy knew that the aliens had to get inside of the ship one way, but maybe they were able to make the entrance disappear once they were all in. Since they couldn't find the entrance, Puggy called them back.

Puggy told Mannie that this was a job that only he could do. Puggy noticed a small control panel on the side of the spaceship. If Mannie opened it and rewired it a little, Puggy knew that he'd be able to reroute the ship to go back to where they came from. Puggy also knew if Mannie used his advanced technology that Mannie would be able to make the ship stop working once the aliens were back in space.

Puggy turned to the other animals and told them to hurry back to the house where Zork and Cyze were trapped and to bring them back there. All of the dogs left together in a hurry. Puggy knew if there were any humans left around, if they saw many dogs running down the street with suits of metal armor, they probably would have fainted in their spots. It took the dogs ten minutes, but they all came back with Zork and Cyze still disguised as George and Kevin. Puggy barked loudly at them.

"Hmph! We're not afraid of you; you're just an average mutt." Cyze said breathless. The animals had manhandled them and treated them like they weren't their creators. When Cyze and Zork saw the dogs returning to them, they thought that they had somehow regained control. However, when they had been recaptured, they knew that the aliens had lost. Even though, their plans had failed, Cyze still remained arrogant.

Puggy barked again and the animals looked at Zork and Cyze with red eyes, they shivered in fear. Zork sighed, knowing that there was nothing else left to do. "Leave my body!" Zork shouted and turned back to normal. A blur flew passed Puggy's eyes and he was shocked to see the human that Zork had taken over laying on the ground.

"Fine!" Cyze shouted angrily. "Leave my body!" the human laid unconscious onto the ground. Puggy and Mannie howled in victory. The animals worked together and stuck Zork's and Cyze's bodies to the spaceship and Mannie sent them flying back into space. When Mannie landed back onto the ground, he ran back over to Puggy and they rubbed their faces against each other. They had won!

Chapter Seven

The weeks that followed that were long and hard. Mannie had managed to hypnotize the humans and had them help Mannie, Puggy, and the modified animals clean up the city. They rebuild homes, fixed light poles and re-cemented the ground. After a while, they had the city back to normal, minus the few trees that were missing.

Each of the animals placed the humans back safely into their own homes and into their beds. Puggy told Mannie to erase their memories of the events that had happened. Mannie made it seem like they had some weird dream that they would have forgotten about once they had woken up.

After all of the humans were back inside their homes, Puggy, Mannie and the modified animals met back in front of Puggy's house. It was time for the dogs to change back to normal.

Puggy thought that if drinking coffee had taken away his modifications, pouring the coffee onto the animals' modification would melt them off of them. Puggy was right! The liquid ate through their modifications and their red eyes went back to normal colors.

The dogs looked at one another, confused to how they had gotten there. Apparently somehow their memories were tampered with once the modifications were gone. Puggy barked, telling them that they were free to go and in confusion, the animals turned in the direction of their homes. Puggy turned towards Mannie, it was his turn.

Puggy felt bad that Mannie had to drink the liquid and get sick, but it needed to be done. A world with modified animals should not exist. Mannie nodded his head in understanding and drunk the contents. He immediately began feeling sick, but Puggy was there for him. Picking the small dog up into his mouth by the fur on Mannie's back, he ran in the direction of Mannie's home.

It was still night when Puggy got back to his house. He went straight into the bedroom and jumped onto the bed. He looked back at Bill lovingly. Puggy, Mannie, and the animals had managed to stop the aliens from achieving their goals.

In the process, they were able to save Bill, who Puggy cared for deeply. Lying down onto the bed, Puggy closed his eyes to get a much needed rest. Before Puggy's consciousness was taken into dream world, he heard Bill's sleepy voice.

"Thank you."

Charlie Publishing

A Note About The Author

Amma Lee was a very imaginative child. Starting with picture books at the age of five, she always loved to read and spent countless hours turning the pages of books. She imagined herself in every picture and made up new stories for every book.

Through her middle school years, she devoured every book she could find. She read everything from princess stories to adventure stories that were written for boys. She loved them all!

Now that she's an adult she loves writing for children of all ages and she still reads children's books when no one is looking. She has been writing full time for five years and has never been happier.

Feel free to contact at **charliepublishing@gmail.com**

56518164R00029

Made in the USA
Lexington, KY
23 October 2016